Dear Parent:
Your child's love of reading starts here!

Every child learns to read in a different way and at his or her own speed. Some go back and forth between reading levels and read favorite books again and again. Others read through each level in order. You can help your young reader improve and become more confident by encouraging his or her own interests and abilities. From books your child reads with you to the first books he or she reads alone, there are I Can Read Books for every stage of reading:

SHARED READING
Basic language, word repetition, and whimsical illustrations, ideal for sharing with your emergent reader

BEGINNING READING
Short sentences, familiar words, and simple concepts for children eager to read on their own

READING WITH HELP
Engaging stories, longer sentences, and language play for developing readers

READING ALONE
Complex plots, challenging vocabulary, and high-interest topics for the independent reader

ADVANCED READING
Short paragraphs, chapters, and exciting themes for the perfect bridge to chapter books

I Can Read Books have introduced children to the joy of reading since 1957. Featuring award-winning authors and illustrators and a fabulous cast of beloved characters, I Can Read Books set the standard for beginning readers.

A lifetime of discovery begins with the magical words **"I Can Read!"**

Visit www.icanread.com for information
on enriching your child's reading experience.

ADVENTURES OF SPLAT THE CAT

Splat the Cat: Good Night, Sleep Tight
Text and illustrations © 2011 by Rob Scotton

Splat the Cat: Splat the Cat Sings Flat
Text and illustrations © 2011 by Rob Scotton

Splat the Cat and the Duck with No Quack
Text and illustrations © 2011 by Rob Scotton

Splat the Cat Takes the Cake
Text and illustrations © 2012 by Rob Scotton

Splat the Cat: The Name of the Game
Text and illustrations © 2012 by Rob Scotton

HarperCollins Publishers® and I Can Read Books® are registered trademarks.

ISBN 978-1-4351-5062-1

Manufactured in Dong Guan City, China
Lot #:
15 16 17 18 19 SCP 5 4 3
08/15

I Can Read!™

Adventures of
Splat the Cat

based on the creation of
Rob Scotton

HARPER
An Imprint of HarperCollinsPublishers

Adventures of
Splat the Cat

Table of Contents

For Theo and Scarlet—keep on singing!
—R.S.

Splat the Cat
Sings Flat

Based on the bestselling books
by **Rob Scotton**

Cover art by Rob Scotton

Text by Chris Strathearn

Interior illustrations by Robert Eberz

Splat the cat goes to Cat School.

Splat likes to take Seymour.

Seymour is Splat's pet mouse.

Seymour rides in Splat's hat.

One morning,

Splat's teacher had big news.

She asked all the cats

to sit on the big red mat.

Seymour sat in Splat's hat.

12

"All of you will sing
on Parents' Night,"
Mrs. Wimpydimple said.
"If your singing is loud,
your parents will be proud."

"Will lots of parents be there?"
asked Splat.

"Yes. All the parents,"
said Mrs. Wimpydimple.

"Gulp!" said Splat.

MUSIC

Splat's tail wiggled wildly.

Splat was worried.

Splat was shy.

"I can't sing," said Splat.

"Can you meow?" asked his teacher.

"I forget how to meow," said Splat.

"Can you hum?" asked his teacher.

"I even forget how to hum,"

said Splat.

"That's okay, Splat,"
said Mrs. Wimpydimple.
"I will help you sing.
We will all help you sing."

Mrs. Wimpydimple sang first.

"La-la-la!" she sang.

The cats on the mat began to sing.

All except Splat.

"Now you try, Splat,"
said Mrs. Wimpydimple.
Splat opened his mouth.
Nothing came out.

"You can do it, Splat,"
said his teacher.
Splat tried hard,
but all that came out
was a little squeak.

Splat looked at Seymour.

Seymour was brave.

He was a mouse

in a room full of cats.

Splat could be brave, too.

Splat opened his mouth again.

"La!" sang Splat.

The note was loud.

It was long.

And it was very, very flat!

The cats on the mat went wild.

Splat was not trying to be funny,

but he was funny anyway.

"Sing just like that!"
said Mrs. Wimpydimple.
"You will be the star
with a mouse in his hat!"
"Maybe," said Splat.

Splat went home after school.

"What if I forget my part?"

Splat asked Mom and Dad.

"You won't forget,"

they said to Splat.

"Maybe I will forget,"

said Splat.

Splat put Seymour on his head.

Splat's tail wiggled

and Seymour jiggled.

Splat sang "la!"

The note still came out flat.

"Maybe I won't forget,"
said Splat.

Soon it was Parents' Night.

All the parents came

to Splat's classroom.

The class stood on the big red mat.

"Let's begin!" said Mrs. Wimpydimple.

The class started to sing.

"La-la-la!" sang the cats.

But Splat stayed quiet.

He waited for his turn.

31

Mrs. Wimpydimple gave Splat a nod.

Splat was ready.

Seymour jumped onto Splat's head.

Seymour was ready, too.

Splat's tail wiggled wildly.

Splat opened his mouth very wide.

"La!" sang Splat,

and the note was flat.

It was very flat and very loud.

He opened his mouth even wider.

"LA!" sang Splat.

Then he opened his mouth

as wide as it could go.

"LAAA!" sang Splat,

and he fell off the mat.

SPLAT!

The class giggled.

The parents laughed.

And Splat laughed

the loudest of all.

"You were the star!"

said Splat's mom.

"We are very proud of you,"

said Splat's dad.

"Splat was the cat's meow!"
said Mrs. Wimpydimple.

Splat was happy.

"Guess what," said Splat.

"I didn't forget to sing flat!

I forgot to be shy."

Mom and Dad hugged Splat.

"We love our cat who sings flat."

Splat the Cat
Good Night, Sleep Tight

Based on the bestselling books
by **Rob Scotton**

Cover art by Rob Scotton

Text by Natalie Engel

Interior illustrations by Robert Eberz

Splat was happy.

It was almost night.

He was getting ready

to camp under the moonlight!

"Everything is just right,"
Splat told his mom.
"I have my sleeping bag.
I have my flashlight."

"And I have a surprise,"
said Splat's mom.
"Let's go outside."

Mom and Splat

went into the garden.

They pulled back the tent flaps.

Splat peered inside the tent.

Two sets of eyes peered back.

"Say hello to Spike and Plank,"

said Splat's mom.

"They are camping here tonight!"

Splat felt his whiskers

wobble with fright.

"Mom," whispered Splat,

"I don't like Spike."

"You might like him better

if you spent some time together,"

said Splat's mom.

"You'll see.

Everything will be just right."

"I'm hungry," said Spike.

"What did you bring

for me to eat?"

"I have some fish cakes,"

Splat said.

"Yum," said Spike.

He gobbled them up in delight.

"Look," said Splat.

"The stars are so bright.

I see at least a million."

"I see seventy-one," said Plank.

"I see nothing," said Spike,

"but two silly cats

looking at the moonlight."

"It's getting late," said Splat.

"Let's try to sleep."

But Plank could not rest.

"My sleeping bag

is much too tight," he said.

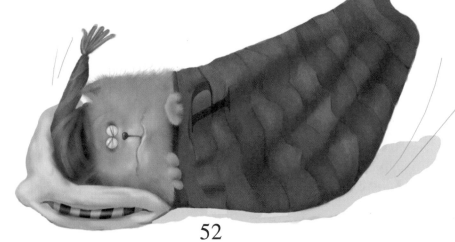

Plank tossed. He turned.

He struggled, stretched, and strained.

RRRIP!

"You're welcome," said Spike.

Splat was just about to fall asleep

when something felt wrong.

He saw a dark shadow

creep up the tent wall.

"Run for your lives!"

Splat shouted

with all his might.

SPLAT!

"Oh my."

Spike laughed.

"Did I give you a fright?"

"What's the big deal?" said Spike.

"Everything is all right."

Splat did not think so.

But he was too tired

to pick a fight.

One by one,

Splat's whiskers drooped.

One by one,

his eyes shut tight.

Suddenly, Spike sprang up.

"What's wrong?" said Splat.

"There's something strange

crawling up my leg!" yelled Spike.

"Mommy!" screamed Spike.

He scrambled out of his sleeping bag.

He stumbled out of the tent.

When Spike took flight,
he took the whole tent
down with him.

"Oh, Seymour!" said Splat.

"It was just you."

"It's all right, Spike!

Come back!" said Splat and Plank.

"We will protect each other

for the rest of the night."

"Promise?" sniffled Spike.

"Promise," said Splat.

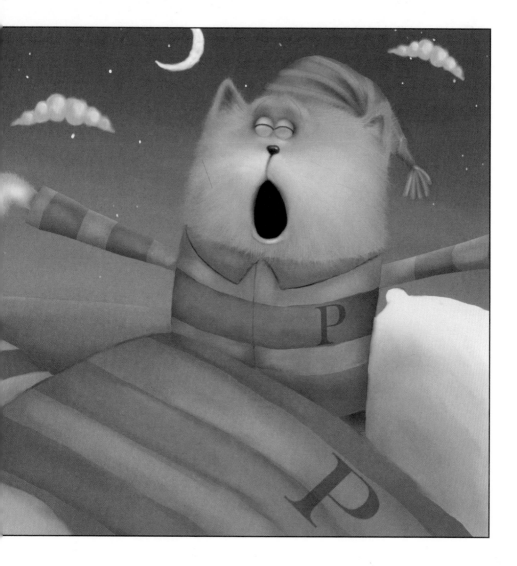

"Now good night," said Splat.

"Sleep tight," said Plank.

"See you in the morning light,"
said Spike.

For three friends

who camped out that night,

everything turned out just right.

Splat the Cat
and the Duck with No Quack

Based on the bestselling books
by **Rob Scotton**

Cover art and text by Rob Scotton

Interior illustrations by Robert Eberz

Splat's bike went clickity clack
as he rode along a bumpy track
to Cat School.

Suddenly, the wheel of the bike
got stuck in a crack.

With a whack and a smack,

Splat tumbled onto the track.

Splat found himself nose to beak

with a funny duck.

The funny duck had a little book.

The duck gave Splat a funny look.

"How odd!" said Splat.

This duck was strangely quiet.

"A duck lacking in quacking,"
said Splat.

"That's not right!"

"Don't worry, Duck," said Splat.

"You must be lost.

I'll take you back to the pond.

I will help you

get your quack back."

Splat picked up the duck

with the little book

and put both in his backpack.

"Take care in there," said Splat.

"And don't sit on

my fish-stick snack."

Splat put his backpack back on,
got on his bike,
and set off again
along the bumpy track
toward the pond.

Duck Pond

Fish Market

Cat School

Splat's bike
went clickity clickity clack
clack clack.

Splat stopped by the pond
and opened his backpack.
Duck popped out,
looked about,
then popped back in again.

"Maybe Duck isn't lost," Splat said.

"Mrs. Wimpydimple

will know what to do."

And Splat wobbled his way

back on the track to Cat School.

When Splat got to school,
he parked his bike
in the bike-rack shack
and dropped his backpack
on the bumpy track.

Duck looked out from a crack
in Splat's backpack.
Duck saw Spike's silly grin
and had a panic attack.

Duck jumped out
of Splat's backpack.
"Duck! Duck!" yelled Splat.

"Where? Where?" yelled Plank,
looking blank.

Too late . . .

SPLURF!

The duck with the little book
sat on Plank's head.
"No quack!" said Splat.
"No quack?" asked Spike
"No quack?" asked Plank.
"No quack!" said Splat.

"A duck lacking in quacking,"

said Spike and Plank.

"That's not right."

"Maybe Duck is hungry," said Spike.

Spike took the fish-stick snack

from Splat's backpack

and gave it to Duck.

But Duck didn't bite.

So Spike ate the fish-stick

snack himself.

"Maybe Duck is sad and needs to be cheered up," said Plank. Plank made a funny face.

Duck didn't laugh.

Duck didn't even grin.

Plank's funny face stayed stuck.

89

"I know, I know!" said Kitten.

"Duck needs a bow

with a little pink dress to match.

That will bring Duck's quack back."

But the bow and the dress

were not a success.

Duck's beak stayed firmly closed.

"Mrs. Wimpydimple will know

what to do," said Splat.

Mrs. Wimpydimple looked at the duck.

"A duck lacking in quacking?"

she asked.

"How very odd.

But the answer must be simple,"

said Mrs. Wimpydimple.

"I will examine this duck
with the little book,"
said Mrs. Wimpydimple.
She played some music
to test Duck's ears.

Duck danced a merry duck dance.

"Duck's hearing is all right.

Maybe the problem

is Duck's eyesight,"

said Mrs. Wimpydimple.

Mrs. Wimpydimple pointed to a chart.

Duck just looked blank.

She looked closely at Duck.

"Hmmm . . . I see," she said.

"But I don't think Duck does."

Mrs. Wimpydimple put her glasses
on Duck's beak.

Duck blinked.

Duck opened the book
and started to read out loud.

As he read, Duck began to quack.

"Quack . . . quack, quack . . ."

Followed by a "quack, quack, quack."

"Hooray for Duck!"

cheered the helpful cats.

Duck's quack was back.

And that was that.

Splat the Cat
Takes the Cake

Based on the bestselling books by Rob Scotton

Cover art by Rob Scotton

Text by Amy Hsu Lin

Interior illustrations by Robert Eberz

Splat the cat

sat watching *Super Cat* on TV.

It was his favorite show.

This time, brave Super Cat
was saving his tiny town
from an awful earthquake!

Splat said, "I want to be

a brave hero, too.

Eek! Look out—a snake!

Seymour, I'll save you!"

So Splat saved Seymour

from a sneaky snake.

104

But he forgot to beware

of his mango milkshake . . .

SPLAT!

"That's that!" exclaimed Dad.

"No more Super Cat.

No more TV."

Pfft!

"No more TV?" Splat groaned.

"No more TV!" said his mom.

"Why not take a bike ride to the lake?"

"Yes, I could use a break," said Splat.

Splat took off on his bike.

Riding helped him shake

his mango milkshake mistake.

On his way to the lake,

Splat saw a big sign.

A clever thought crossed his mind.

He could bake a TV-winning cake.

109

Splat never made it to the lake.

Instead, he sped home

to bake his cake.

He opened Mom's cake book

and looked and flipped.

But no cake in that book

had the tippy-top look

of a super first-prize cake.

So Splat said, "I'll bake

my own super-duper cake.

One that nobody else can make!"

Splat said, "Let's see.

I'll need a large pan or two,

or maybe three."

Splat put in
all the things he needed
to bake a super-duper cake.

Splat said to Seymour,

"More cake flour

makes more cake power!"

Then he added one more thing.

The cake was now ready to bake.

But that last thing Splat added

was a big, BIG mistake!

SPLAT!

Now there was no cake.

And there was a BIG mess.

Splat was too tired to bake
another cake.
He went to bed thinking,
"How will I win the TV?
What would Super Cat do?"

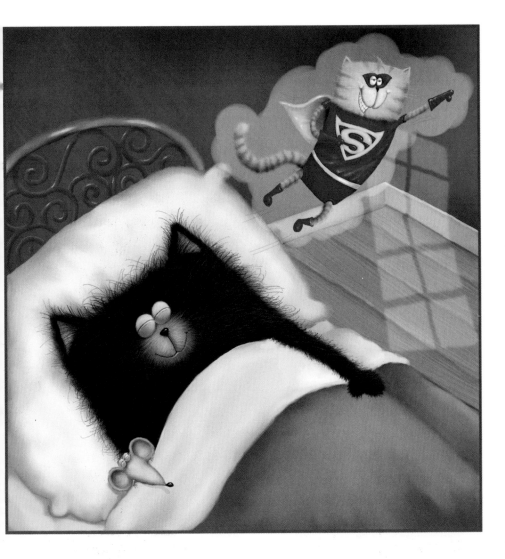

Then Splat dreamed

of Super Cat.

When Splat woke up

he knew what to do

and how to bake his super cake.

At the contest, Splat was ready.

Spike was there with his cake.

Kitten was there with her cake.

Plank had baked a cake, too.

Spike's cake was wider.

Kitten's cake was prettier.

Plank's cake was taller.

Was Splat's cake super enough?

CONTEST!

SUPER CAT!

The judges looked closely
at every cake baked.
They tasted the cakes.
They talked together.

Then one judge said,

"Our top judge will now

award the Super Cake prize."

Surprise!

The top judge was really Super Cat!

"Splat the cat takes the cake!"
said Super Cat.

"I mean he takes the TV."

Splat was very happy.

When he got home

he said, "Now it's time

to watch *Super Cat*!"

"It's you who takes the cake,

Super Cat," whispered Splat.

Splat the Cat
The Name of the Game

Based on the bestselling books by Rob Scotton

Cover art by Rob Scotton

Text by Amy Hsu Lin

Interior illustrations by Robert Eberz

Spike and Plank were

at Splat's house to play games.

"Let's play Mouse, Mouse, Cat,"
said Splat.

"I'll go first," Spike said.

"Mouse . . . mouse . . . cat!" he said.

Spike tagged Splat.

Splat tripped

when he chased Spike.

SPLAT!

"What a shame,"

said Splat's little sister.

"So sad, too bad.

You lost the game!"

"Let's play hide-and-seek!

I'll be it," said Plank.

Splat said, "Don't peek!"

Plank began to count.

Spike went to hide.

Splat hid behind a curtain.

Plank found Splat right away.

"That spot was tame.

So sad, too bad.

You lost the game!"

said Little Sis.

No one could find Spike.

"Good spot, Spike!" said Plank.

"You win!" said Splat.

"I want to play," said Little Sis.

"Fine. You're it," said Splat.

Splat, Spike, and Plank went to hide.

This time Splat found a great spot:

a sooty fireplace with no flame.

Splat's nose itched.

"ACHOO!"

Little Sis

found him right away.

"That's lame," she said.

"So sad, too bad.

You lost the game!"

Little Sis found

Spike and Plank, too.

"Yippee! I win," she said.

"I get all the fame."

"Why don't I ever win?" Splat said.

"You almost did," said Spike.

"Maybe the next game," said Plank.

"So sad, too bad.

You lost the game!"

said Little Sis.

Splat shook his head.

"No more games," he said.

"But that's why we came,"

said Spike.

"How about Go Fish?" Plank said.

"Or Freeze Cat?" Spike said.

"Or jump rope?" said Little Sis.

"You can play without me," said Splat.

Splat started to play by himself.

Spike, Plank, and Little Sis

played together, too.

Playing alone was not much fun.

"Now this is a shame.

It's tame and lame!" said Splat.

"This isn't the same," said Spike.

"Not without Splat," said Plank.

"No, it isn't," said Little Sis.

"What are you playing?

And can I play, too?" asked Splat.

"Any game you like," said Plank.

"Play with us again!" said Spike.

"Please, Splat?" asked Little Sis.

"Okay," Splat said with a smile.

"Let's play hide-and-seek

just one more time."

"I'll be it," said Spike.

He began to count.

This time, Splat thought of

the best place of all to hide.

Spike found Plank first.

Then he found Little Sis.

Then the friends looked for Splat,

but they couldn't find him.

Plank said, "Splat, come out!"

Spike said, "Splat, where are you?"

Little Sis said, "Come out,

come out, wherever you are."

"Here I am!

I'm in the frame!" said Splat.

"You win!" said Spike.

"You win!" said Plank.

"You won the game!" said Little Sis.

"I win because I have

the best friends," said Splat.